ZEE ZEE ZOMBIE
DENNY PHILLIPS

Zee Zee Zombie

Denny Phillips

Published by Dee Phillips, 2024.

Zee Zee Zombie

Chapter One

THERE WAS SOMETHING about living in a world on the brink of catastrophic collapse, a world just recently ravaged by disaster of potentially apocalyptic proportions that just rewired the human brain to wake up at just the right times, without the need for deeply infuriating, headache-inducing alarm clocks. Before all of this, getting out of bed early in the morning was a near impossible task for Zebediah Ezekial with his waking hours usually defaulted to about ten or eleven in the morning, and now, he was sitting upright in bed at five in the morning, before there'd even been a crack of sunlight in the sky.

Zebediah—or Zee Zee, as his friends and colleagues had taken to calling him—had never seen the importance of a fixed morning routine prior to the collapse of the world as he knew it, but now, a routine was a necessity. Not only was it important that he did specific things in the morning for his safety, it was also a great away to keep his mind intact—in times like this where the mind was at its most fragile, it was incredibly important to take steps that could help him retain his sanity, although he imagined there were people who would question if he'd ever been sane.

After five minutes of waiting for his mind to gain some focus and clarity after waking, he rose off his bed, slid his feet into his slippers and ambled his way towards the bathroom, first brushing his teeth clean and flossing to take care of any residual dirt that might have been left in there and then he climbed into the decontamination shower and set the shower's timer to ten minutes. Decontamination showers weren't pleasant in the least, with the strong scent of antiseptic overwhelming his nose every time he took one, a mild burning sensation spreading across the entirety of his body as he was 'purified' of any contaminants. For ten minutes, he had to try to concentrate on things other than the despicable scent and burning of the powerful antiseptic within the water.

After his shower, he made his way to the storage unit in his bedroom, unlocked the combination lock, and pulled out an index finger sized vial filled with a purple liquid. He transferred the content of the vial into a syringe, and bit his lips before injecting the protective serum into his body—a serum that had to be administered at 12-hourly intervals, to limit the risk of contracting the infection. These were measures that had all been made necessary as the people on planet Andromeda sought ways to survive the most lethal thing their civilization had ever encountered—the planet's poisoned atmosphere, an atmosphere that infected the people with an extremely lethal, fast-acting virus that was turning Andromedans into mindless, bloodlusty predators.

With the serum administered, Zebediah put on pristine clean clothes, clothes that he'd personally disinfected himself. Once fully clothed, he made his way across his room, to the calendar on the wall and ticked off another day—the 14th of June. Seven months since the Aberration. Seven months since the chemical plant, CosmoChem, set off an explosion that reverberated throughout the entire planet, killing hundreds of thousands of Andromedans and severely wounding thousands more, while also poisoning the planet's atmosphere with an unidentifiable toxin that set off rapid mutations within the Andromedan body, triggering rapid cell decay and altering brain signals, turning Andromedans into mindless predators who became unrecognizable to their families and had to be quarantined or disposed of for public safety.

To combat the Aberration, the Planetary Organization of Health Safety and Sanitization [PO-HSS], a body with some of the finest minds in medicine on the planet had hastily put together the serum that showed signs of helping the infected slow down the spread of their infection and allowed them to retain brain functionality, albeit at a somewhat reduced level. The serum also displayed incredible effectiveness in keeping the uninfected safe from the virus, although it was still early days of the Aberration and no one knew how much longer the serum would remain effective. Zebediah, however, wasn't planning to stick around long enough to find out how much longer it would be until the HSS-Serum ceased to be effective and the virus took over what was left of the planet's populace.

Once he'd had his breakfast, he grabbed the rifle he'd stored beneath his bed, slung it across his shoulder, pulled out a backpack containing ammo and a bunch of the tools and equipment he needed for what he was working on, and then exited his cozy little safehouse, ensuring the door was safely sealed shut behind him, the panel on the wall next to it blinking yellow to signify the door had been locked. He climbed onto his bike, brought the engine to life and cast one look around the street—a street populated with safehouses similar to his, with not a single sound coming from any of them. The atmosphere here was filled with a burdening sense of gloom, with not a single other soul in sight. Zebediah was certain there were people sheltered within the safehouses but unlike him, most other Andromedans preferred to remain within the confines of their safehouses, afraid that they faced a risk of infection if they ventured out. He knew the truth, though—he knew it didn't matter if they stayed inside or not, he'd done all the calculations over and over again, he knew the entire planet was on a clock. In months, maybe even weeks, every Andromedan who wasn't infected would be, they'd all be one of those things out there. The Burned. The Crazies. The Yuckheads. The Zombies.

Daylight had started to crack through the sky by the time he brought his bike to a stop forty minutes later, four blocks away from his actual destination—an abandoned warehouse that he'd repurposed into something that was better kept hidden from everyone he didn't trust. Ahead of him was a horde of the zombies, staggering back and forth with weird gargling and snarling sounds coming from them, a yellow goo oozing out of their puffy, bloodshot eyes, their skin peeled off and rotting in places, with flies circling around them. Zebediah cursed under his breath and took a right turn, hoping it was possible to circle around and find a path into the warehouse that wouldn't involve him having to go up against them.

The alternate path into the warehouse had also been crowded by the zombies, staggering back and forth like the other group he'd seen. A frown swept across Zebediah's face as he slowly realized that something had to be wrong, there had to be a reason why so many of them had gathered this close to the warehouse. This couldn't be coincidental—in a post-apocalyptic world, one couldn't run the risk of believing in coincidences. Zebediah gritted his teeth and placed a hand over his rifle, starting to consider his options. He could turn around, head away from the warehouse and return to his safehouse but he was on a clock, he had to finish what he was working on. And if he tried to shoot his way out of this, there was every chance he'd only attract more of the zombies.

"Come on, Zeb, use that beautiful brain of yours," he muttered to himself, scanning his surroundings. Trying to force his way through the horde and into the warehouse would see him either get ripped apart to bloodied meaty bits, or would see him become one of them. And turning around wasn't at all a suitable option for him. He was getting in that warehouse today.

He got so lost in his thoughts, trying to figure out a plan, that he didn't realize a number of the zombies were already creeping up on him from behind, and it was only when one of them launched itself at him, missing by inches that he realized he was in trouble. He turned around, saw the group that had somehow snuck up on him and immediately put his foot to the pedal, putting some distance between himself and the zombies.

"What the bloody hell is going on here today?" he muttered and slapped against the bike's handle in frustration. "I've got to get in there!"

A dangerous idea popped into Zebediah's head, one that would most certainly result in his untimely demise if it didn't go as planned but it was the only thing he could think of that would get the zombies away from the warehouse and provide him with a clear path into the place.

He mulled the plan over and over, and when he couldn't come up with anything better, he decided to go through with it, turning off the silent mode on his bike and switching on the auto-pilot feature. On the GPS, he set for the bike to just speed in a straight line, a path that would eventually bring it crashing into one of the abandoned homes in the area.

He climbed off the bike, turned on the radio mounted on the handlebar and flipped a button that immediately put the auto-pilot into effect, with the bike speeding away from him as music blasted from the mounted speakers. The zombies snarled and tilted their heads in the direction of the bike, roaring before breaking into pursuit of the noise that they believed to be coming from a potential meal. These things couldn't see, at least not very well, so they hunted with their senses of smell and hearing, and seeing as the decontamination shower left behind a powerful smell that masked scents, the only thing the zombies could pick up on right now was sound.

With the zombies in pursuit of his bike, Zebediah broke into a sprint in the direction of the warehouse, his rifle slung across the shoulder, backpack in his left hand, the contents of the backpack banging against each other as he moved as fast as he could, silently hoping that the rather sensitive items within the backpack didn't react terribly and disintegrate him. Ahead of him, a few more zombies popped out of an alley just before the warehouse with their sights focused on him, snarling as they limped towards him, hands outstretched, their jaws hanging off loosely, puffy red eyes oozing revolting amounts of goo. These hadn't gone in pursuit of the bike like the others and that meant he'd have to take care of them himself. He dropped his backpack to the ground and grabbed his rifle, turning the safety off with a click and training the weapon's sights on one of the braindead creatures. Before all of this, before the Aberration, he'd had no idea how to hold a gun correctly, let alone shoot it but in the months since the world descended into nightmarish madness, marksmanship was a skill he'd have been stupid to not pick up. And like most other things he did, he was very good at it.

With no hesitation, he pulled back on the trigger, a smile spreading across his face as the bullet took the zombie's clean off, the headless corpse dropping to the ground instantly. He aimed at the next, and made a clean headshot yet again, and he replicated the same headshot with the next. That was the most efficient way to take care of these darn things—by blowing their heads right off, and that was exactly what he did to all seven of them, blasting their heads clean off their rotting bodies before picking his backpack off the ground and continuing towards the warehouse at a quick pace. He had to get there before the zombies that had gone in pursuit of the bike started to head back in this direction. Once he was inside, he could seal himself in there and work on his project for the rest of the day. By the time he was done, the number of zombies out on the streets would have grossly reduced.

Once he reached the warehouse's sealed doors, he dipped a hand into the pocket of his denim trousers, fumbling for the keycard he needed to open up the doors, cursing under his breath as he felt empty wrappers of gums, coins, spare bullets, everything except the card he was searching for. Panic had started to set in as he feared he may have left the card back at the safehouse when he searched his other pocket and found the card there, a sigh of relief escaping his mouth. He pulled the card out and swiped, but there was a repeated beeping sound as the door rejected the card.

"No, no, no, don't you dare do this right now!" he yelled and pounded a fist against the door before swiping the card once more, being greeted with more declining beeps. "No, no, come on, damnit!"

He inhaled deeply, calming his nerves and then swiped the card slowly this time. There was a ding sound and the red light on the door blinked once then turned green, and just as he reached out his hands to push the doors open, a loud voice came from just across the warehouse, startling him so much so that he was certain he could have jumped out of his own skin.

"Zee Zee!" the feminine voice came from across the warehouse. The voice was instantly recognizable—it was Artemis Hunt, a friend slash colleague of his who often helped him acquire resources for his project. "Don't open the doors! Run!"

Zebediah heard far too late, since he'd already pushed the doors open, and as soon as he saw what awaited him behind the door, he understood what the warning had been for. The warehouse had been packed full with dozens of them, all stumbling over each other, snarling and clawing at the air, and the moment he opened the doors, all of their attention turned to him and their snarling grew enraged as they started to charge at him.

"Oh fuck!" he yelled and grabbed his gun, preparing to open fire but firm hands grabbed him by the collar from behind and yanked, pulling him with incredible force and moving at incredible speed, dragging him across the street, into one of the abandoned buildings and pushing him against a wall immediately, a finger being tightly pressed against his lips, signifying he had to remain quiet.

Artemis shut the door to the abandoned building, bolted it shot and then slid a very heavy-looking table in front of the door with ridiculous ease. Zebediah swirled around to glare at the towering, hulking man that had dragged him into the building—Tank, as they'd nicknamed him, and for easily identifiable reasons. He wore a tank top, revealing his bulked up arms that had various scars running along them, guns and grenades strapped around his waist with more holstered just above his knees.

"Someone mind telling me why the hell there's a bunch of those things running around my damn warehouse?!" Zebediah hissed angrily but Tank simply pressed a finger against his lips again, gesturing for him to remain quiet, nodding in the direction of the windows within the building.

"Any noises and they'll all come in here," Tank whispered, although his voice was so thick and deep and booming that his whispering sounded like normal speech. "We gotta lay low here for a bit. Vic and Scar are upstairs, looking out."

"And Tom?"

Both Tank and Artemis stared at Zebediah grimly, their faces falling, with Artemis scratching against the back of her palm like she always did when she was distressed or anxious. She looked into Tank's eyes then let out a sigh and returned her gaze to Zebediah before finally providing a response. "He's in the warehouse."

Zebediah looked confused. "I'm sorry, what?"

"Recon and Obtain went south, Zee Zee," Tank explained. "We went in search of the andrium fuels just like you asked, so we could power up your little baby, the Xtrium military site that you told us would be abandoned and have what we needed turned out to be a damn nest for those damn crazies."

"Wait, it's my fault now that you got Tom killed?" Zebediah queried, squaring up to Tank. "This is all on me now?"

"Tom isn't dead," Artemis said quickly. "He can't be."

"I don't know if this is your first day on this planet but you just said he was in a warehouse filled with a horde of those things," Zebediah said, turning around to face her. "From your experience, anyone ever survived being around that many of them?"

"Tom will," Artemis said optimistically. "He's different. He lured them in there so we could get to safety, but we're going to try to get him out of there. He'll make it through this."

"You know my life's work is within that warehouse, right?" Zebediah asked. "The only way we survive this damn apocalypse is within that warehouse and you thought it was a good idea to lead those things right to it?"

"Relax, if it's damaged, you can fix it. You got a big brain, don't you? Not like we're in a hurry or anything," Tank grunted.

"We are in a hurry!" Zebediah yelled. "Have you not listened to anything I've been saying over the past couple of weeks? I've done the math, I've done the chemistry, I've done the biology, I've done the physics, I've done everything! In less than fifteen days, everyone on this planet is going to be either dead or one of those damn things. We need the SLR-Titanic up and running ASAP or everything I've done for seven months, everything we've done, it'll all be for nothing."

"Well, what's your plan? You want us to head out there and engage in a brawl with all of those things? Because the only way that ends is with all of us infected, and if you get infected and become one of those things then the planet's good as dead. You're our ticket out of here, and I'd much rather see the ship scratched up than see you scratched up," Tank growled.

Zebediah sighed. "How do we get Tom out of there?"

Before Tank could respond, gunfire came from above them, from Vic and Scar. Tank grunted and reached for a gun and started heading upstairs but he was only halfway up the stairs when the windows shattered as a horde of the zombies charged straight through, hitting the ground with a loud thud, snarling loudly as they started to advance towards Zebediah and Artemis.

"Oh, for fuck's sake," Artemis growled and she lifted her shotgun, aimed it in the direction of the zombies, switched the safety off with a click and smiled as she prepared to fire.

"Artemis, no!" Tank yelled, but it was too late. There was a loud BANG! as she fired, blasting off a zombie's head and sending yellow goo and decayed brain matter spraying in every direction, and then another BANG! as she fired again, causing Zebediah to wince in pain.

More snarling sounds came from outside the house as fists pounded and clawed against the door, with more of the creatures crawling in through the windows. Hurried footsteps came from above them and Vic and Scar came into visibility at the foot of the stairs, frantic expressions on their faces.

"They're here," Vic said, wiping sweat off his panicked face.

"They're all here," Scar added, brushing her scarlet-colored hair out of her face. "We're trapped."

Chapter Two

IT WAS PANDEMONIUM. All of them had backed up against each other, frantic expressions on their faces, their outfits soaked with sweat and stained with goo and blood from the zombies as they were stuck in a loop of firing and reloading their weapons as quickly as they could, determined to prevent any of the flesh craving creatures from getting too close to them, with the major problem being that the loud gunfire was attracting every zombie within a two-mile radius to them. A major scare came when something powerful slammed into the door and managed to push it open slightly, prompting but Artemis and Zebediah to push the table against the door, shutting it quickly. Zebediah didn't feel any relief after shutting the door again considering it was only a matter of time till they ran out of ammunition and were completely overwhelmed by the relentless monsters, and he had no doubt that by now, there were more than just grunts out there—hulkers and runners would no doubt have been attracted to the building by now.

"Zee Zee, use your beautiful brain damnit!" Tank yelled as he shoved a gun right into the mouth of one of the zombies and fired, the bullet blasting the creature's head off and ripping straight through the head of the three other zombies behind it. Tank let out a maniacal laugh, rolled his gun in his hands and continued shooting with frightening precision but he too must have known that it wasn't something he could keep up much longer. Tank and the others had been out here far longer than Zebediah had been and their fatigue was slowly becoming visible. If Zebediah didn't come up with a plan to get all of them away from there, the abandoned house would soon become one rather enormous coffin for all of them.

"Zee Zee?!" Scar yelled as she reached into the quiver strapped to her back, pulled out an arrow, placed it against the string of her bow and fired into the midst of the zombies, the arrow exploding the moment it hit the ground and sending zombie guts flying in every direction, with

Zebediah wiping a rotten intestine off his face with a look of disgust. Back when all of this had started, a situation like this would have seen Zebediah puking for hours on end but he'd long since gotten used to all of the rather traumatizing gore that came with being forced to survive in an apocalyptic world.

Zebediah had one plan and it was incredibly risky, but if it worked, he'd be able to get to the warehouse, they'd all be able to get there and once they were there, they could seal themselves in. The zombies wouldn't be able to force their way into the warehouse since he'd installed high-security doors months ago, and sealed all of the windows. He just hoped the others would be onboard with his plan.

"Zebediah Ezekial, you come up with a good idea right now or I'll blow my own brains out!" Vic yelled as he wiped the blood that had splattered onto his arm off his denim jacket, and started to reload his gun immediately. "Hurry up the gears in your head, buddy."

"I'm a rocket scientist, not some bloody war veteran with strategies and whatnot," Zebediah hissed as he aimed his gun at a zombie donning military uniform ripped in many places and took the creature's head clean off with a precise shot. "But I do have an idea. And it's incredibly suicidal, especially if there's runners out there."

"What's the idea?" Artemis asked. "I'll take anything at this point."

"We set charges here," Zebediah responded, and for a second, all of the gunfire came to a halt as they stared at him like he'd gone nuts. A zombie lunged at Tank but he caught the creature perfectly in midair and ripped its head off with ease then hurled the head with force at another zombie and tossed the headless body to the ground.

"Are you out of your mind?" Tank queried.

"Hear me out," Zebediah said, then pointed at various spots downstairs. "We place the charges at those spots and everyone heads upstairs. Well, not everyone. Someone stays down here to open the door to give them an entrance so they stop circling round and surrounding us, once enough of them are in here and we have a window of opportunity, we, uhhh, we jump. And then we run like crazy, back to the warehouse and we seal ourselves in there. Then, of course, we detonate the charges and bring this place down on all the zombies that'll have gathered in here."

"No!" Scar made her disapproval known with a yell then fired another arrow into the head of a zombie that had just climbed in through the window, the arrow exploding immediately. "Are you mental? What's to say they don't get to us before we jump, or as soon as we've jumped."

"They're drawn to smells and sounds," Zebediah muttered, then reached into his backpack and pulled out a dagger. Artemis's eyes widened in terror but before she could say anything, Zebediah made a deep cut in the palm of his left hand and walked around the building, staining all of the spots he'd pointed to earlier with his blood. The snarling outside got louder, a sign that they'd already picked up on the scent.

"Have you gone nuts?" Tank questioned.

"Start setting the charges," Zebediah ordered. "We're getting the fuck out of here right now."

Artemis scrambled towards the living room where she'd left her backpack, opened it up and started to pull out the explosives stored inside, tossing them to the others who caught it perfectly and started to place them down at the spots that had been marked with Zebediah's blood. Zebediah hurried towards his backpack, pulled out an antiseptic spray and used it on his cut before retrieving a bandage from the backpack and hurriedly wrapping it around the cut. Once that was done, he zipped the backpack close and slung it across his shoulder.

"Ready?" he asked.

"Fuck no, but we ain't got much of a choice now, do we?" Vic muttered and put his gun back in the holster. "Who's getting the door open?"

"I'll do it," Zebediah answered with no hesitation, a fiercely determined expression on his face. "Rest of you head upstairs, and as soon as enough of them are in here, make the jump. All the blood down here should keep them from coming up after us, at least, for a while. It'll be enough time."

"Nuh-uh," Tank shook his head. "We're not risking that. You're the only one who can power up that ship of yours in the warehouse, the only one who can get us off this damn planet. I'll open up the door, you get your beautiful brain upstairs with everyone else."

Zebediah shook his head. "We have no idea if Tom's dead or not, we can't lose someone else. Not someone who's key to our survival like you. Get upstairs, I promise I'll make it to you guys. Plus, I'm sure Scar knows how to work the ship as well as I do."

"You're kidding, right?" Scar snorted. "Your toy looks like alien tech to me."

Tank placed a hand on Zebediah's shoulder gently. "Go. I've got this covered. Trust me. Or I could just haul you upstairs myself, entirely your choice, I guess."

"Tank," Zebediah began but Tank silenced him with a playful—but deeply excruciating—punch to the shoulders.

"Get out of here, Zee Zee," Tank grinned. "Before more of those things get in here. Don't make me make you."

"Come on, we gotta hurry," Vic said, glancing in the direction of a group that had now gathered by the window to their right. Reluctantly, Zebediah started to head towards the stairs, pausing once he was halfway up to give Tank a nod before continuing. Once they were upstairs, they headed towards an opened window and waited, grim expressions on all of their faces. At first, Zebediah tapped his fingers anxiously against the frame of the window and then started to pace back and forth as intense levels of panic started to set in—this was a stupid plan, and he wasn't comfortable with Tank being the one downstairs. It ought to be him, it was his plan, he was the one who was supposed to lay his life on the line for the plan's execution. For months, the people he'd gotten close to had laid their lives down for him because they believed him to be some messiah that would help the Andromedans survive this apocalypse, but if he did fall short while they were this dangerously close to going extinct, then all of those sacrifices would have been for naught.

"Relax, Zee Zee" Artemis spoke gently, placing a hand on his back, her bright blue eyes gazing straight into his caramel-colored eyes. "It's Tank. We all know those things aren't going to kill him. Dude's a...well, he's a tank. He'll be fine."

"It's not just him," Zebediah muttered. "It's everything else. We have no idea if those things damaged the ship while they were in there, and if they did, we don't know the extent of the damage. We've got a little over two weeks left to get off the planet or our people die out completely. Too many people have died for this for me to be a total failure at the end. Jake and Jordan, Shane, Hayden, Maurice...my son," his voice broke off.

"You're not a failure," Artemis said fiercely. "You won't be one. Everyone who gave their lives for this did so because they knew you and they had faith in you. We all have faith in you. You're one of the brightest minds on the planet and the only reason the rest of us are here with you right now is because you saved our lives. You saved my life by building an explosive using your phone, some toothpaste, and a bunch of other stuff I didn't even understand. If anyone's going to save what's left of Andromeda, Zee Zee, it'll be you."

"But the ship..."

"If the ship's broken, you'll fix it and we'll do whatever's necessary to help," Artemis continued. "We'll get everyone off this planet, we will. You just gotta believe and try not to put too much pressure on that beautiful mind of yours."

Zebediah smiled but the smile was very brief since he heard the scratching of wood against wood coming from beneath them. Tank had moved the table. Seconds later, a loud yell came from Tank followed by his hurried footsteps up the stairs. He appeared in the room they were all gathered in and slammed the door shut behind him, using the bolts immediately.

"You okay?" Vic asked, arching one eyebrow over the other as he approached Tank cautiously. "Uh, you didn't get bitten, did you?"

"Only thing I'd let bite me is a hooker at O'Shaughnessy's," Tank joked and hurried towards the window, gazing out onto the street below, the rest of them peeking out too, waiting until enough of the zombies were in the house with them. Once their window of opportunity opened up, they'd seize it and make their way towards the warehouse before setting off the explosives.

"I say we make the jump now," Vic said and had started to climb out the window but Artemis grabbed onto him and pulled him backwards, shaking her head. Of all of them, Artemis was the one who possessed an eerie awareness of space and danger, and if she said it wasn't the right time to jump then there was no one who was going to disagree with her.

"Any moment now," she murmured.

Zebediah's head snapped towards the door as he heard a gentle scratching sound come from behind it, his heart skipping a couple of beats as he picked up on the sound. He gulped and glanced at Artemis. "Uh, they're making their way upstairs already. That door won't hold them out very long."

"Just a moment," Artemis said calmly, shutting her eyes and inhaling deeply, almost like she was judging the danger with her sense of smell—which was eerily good for an Andromedan.

The noises coming from behind the door grew louder, so much so that Zebediah was prepared to ignore Artemis and just jump out the window but when he moved forward, she extended an arm to block him off and shook her head at him. "I need you to trust me, and wait."

A loud growl came from behind the door, the growl of a hulker—a zombie whose mutation had somehow morphed it into a bulking, raging monster with strength far greater than that of other zombies. If there was a hulker out there then this door was only seconds away from behind punched off its hinges.

"Uh, Artemis, not to be a bother but I think we really need to take this leap of suicidal faith right fucking now," Scar hissed and stuck her head out the window, scanning for threats. "I don't see anything out there."

Another loud growl came from just outside the door and something slammed into it with incredible force, knocking the door right off the hinges and sending it crashing to the ground. A hulking monster stood where the door had been, razor-sharp teeth bared at them, the same yellow goo oozing from its puffy red eyes. Long ago, this thing had been an Andromedan like them and now it was...something else. Something less than alive and worse than dead.

"Now!" Artemis yelled.

They all charged out the window, one after the other, dropping to the cold ground below with a hard thud, rolling and immediately breaking into a sprint across the street, back towards the warehouse. Vic jumped last and sprained his foot with the landing, letting out an agonized yell but he still pushed through, sprinting in a limping manner behind all of them, still moving with astonishing speed despite the sprain.

Once they were all through the warehouse's open doors, Zebediah shut them loudly and pounded his fist against the red button that would seal the doors and make sure it couldn't be opened without a keycard. Once the doors were sealed, they all let out sighs of relief and bent over, taking deep breaths before simultaneously bursting into laughter, tears rolling out of Zebediah's eyes as he laughed.

Their relief and joy came far too early though, and when a monstrous growl came from inside the warehouse, they all fell quiet, listening again to be sure their mind wasn't playing tricks on them.

There was total silence for about forty seconds, and just when Zebediah was about to brush the growl off as a trick their mind was playing on them, they heard it again...much louder this time.

And this time, there was more than just a growl. There were heavy footsteps and the uncomfortable sound of lips smacking hungrily.

The sound of a hungry hulker.

Chapter Three

THEY WERE ALL FROZEN IN FEAR. Tank equipped two guns, switching the safety off the both of them while Scar reached into her quiver and drew an arrow, preparing to fire at the hulker as soon as it came into view. Hulkers were a lot stronger than normal zombies but what they possessed in bone-crushing strength, they lacked in speed and mobility. That meant that despite their strength, hulkers were still fairly easy to take down as long as Zeb and the others kept their distance and moved quickly, although it would take far more bullets to take down a hulker than it would to take down a regular.

"Come on out here, yer bloated cannibal!" Tank yelled loudly, his guns aimed at a dark corner of the warehouse. "Come on, then. Don't be shy, I got a couple bullets waiting to introduce themselves to you."

Scar growled and placed the arrow to the string of her bow, drawing back immediately, prepared to fire into the dark but Zebediah extended an arm in front of her, demanding that she wait before firing. They had no idea where the hulker was and he didn't need her doing more damage to his warehouse than was necessary, especially with all of the incredibly sensitive things being stored within the warehouse. Incredibly sensitive things like the enormous spacecraft currently on a huge platform in the middle of the warehouse, although none of them could see the ship right now since Zebediah had always made sure to turn on the ship's cloaking before everyday before he left the warehouse. He didn't need some moron managing to crack the warehouse's security, breaking in and destroying what he'd dedicated his life to building.

"Why isn't it coming out?" Artemis queried, a confused expression on her face. Zombies possessed no measurable intelligence and it was certainly uncharacteristic of them to attempt to be stealthy. If there was a hulker in here, it would have revealed itself by now and tried to devour all of them...but so far, there hadn't been any sign of a hulker, and they hadn't heard its growl for a while now.

"Because there's no hulker," Zebediah muttered and gestured for both Tank and Scar to stand down, the two of them obliging but with some degree of reluctance while Zebediah relaxed his own stance too. "We're just being cruelly pranked by one certain Tomas Tompson."

A chuckle came from the dark and moments later, Tom stepped into visibility, his face bloodied, as were his clothes and hands. His trousers were ripped in multiple places, and his dark blond hair was now caked with dirt, blood and bits of yellow goo, a mischievous grin on his face as he looked at the others. "Man, I got you guys so good," he chuckled again. "Did y'all see the look on Vic's face? Jeez, and Zee Zee, you looked like you were about to shit yourself."

"Haha, funny," Zebediah muttered, and walked towards Tom, with Artemis sprinting past him and reeling Tom into a firm hug before pressing her lips against his. When she pulled away from him, her face had turned red and she looked embarrassed while the grin on Tom's face had only grown wider.

"You okay?" Zebediah asked once he was right in front of Tom, hoping he hadn't been bitten by any of those things. "You look, uh...very...not sure what's the right thing to say here."

"You look a right mess," Tank completed for Zebediah. "All that blood, you didn't get bitten, did ya? Cause if you did, you gotta speak up right now so I can axe that head of yours right off. Never liked that curly head of yours anyways."

Tom flipped the middle finger at Tank then hit him playfully in the shoulder before turning serious and directing his attention to Zebediah. "No bites, but I will still take the serum as a precaution. But I think I'm okay, though. No sharp pain or stinging, no feverish sensation, no pounding head, no bloodlust. None of the symptoms we've discovered over the past few months. But there's something you should know...and err, try not to take my head off when I show you."

Zebediah arched an eyebrow over the other. "Uh, I'm going to need you to explain exactly what you're talking about." Zebediah glanced in the direction of the cloaked spacecraft then back at Tom. "The spaceship isn't damaged, is it? Please tell me those things didn't damage the Solar Titanic."

"Nahh," Tom scratched the back of his head, an awkward expression on his face. "It's a funny story, really."

"You see anyone laughing?" Tank asked.

Tom wiggled a finger at Tank and grinned. "See, that's because I haven't gotten around to the bit where I tell the story to an interested audience. I'm afraid I'm going to have to ask all of you to sit down for this bit. And err, it'd be nice if you gently kicked your weapons a great distance away."

"What happened to the SLR-Titanic, Tom?" Artemis asked.

Tom sighed. "I don't know exactly, really," he answered. "Them damn braindead things were all over this place, a huge number around the ship, a huge number trying to sink their teeth into my spotless skin and as you'd expect, Tom gotta go down with a bang. So I gave 'em hell, except I'm pretty sure that one of the shots I did fire hit the ship, but since it's cloaked, I can't tell just how much damage I might have done to it."

"No, no, no," Zebediah murmured and hurried towards the ship's platform, light strips on the floor lighting up and illuminating the path to the ship. Once he was directly in front of the platform, he placed his hand against the panel which scanned his prints, beeped multiple times and a holographic face identical to his popped up. "ZEB-SLR71, deactivate the cloaking on the ship."

"ZEB-SLR71 recognized," a robotic voice somewhat identical to Zebediah's said. "Zebediah Ezekial. Command accepted. Deactivating cloaking."

Slowly, an enormous glossy black spacecraft came became visible, glowing purple lines running across the length of the ship, it's propulsors highlighted by glowing green lines. Zebediah didn't care much for the stunning beauty of the ship, all he cared about in that moment was the integrity of the spaceship, the spaceship that was their only hope for survival. At first glance, Zebediah couldn't notice anything wrong with the ship and was slowly becoming more relaxed, certain that a bullet couldn't have done much damage to the ship—after all, he'd focused on making the spacecraft as sturdy as it could get since it would have to withstand the crushing demands of long-distance space travel at FTL speeds.

"Titan, run full diagnostics on SLR-Titanic," he ordered the AI.

"Running diagnostics. Estimated time of completion: twenty seconds."

The next twenty seconds were easily the most anxious Zebediah had been in a while as he paced back and forth, biting his nails frantically as the others looked on fearfully, with Tom tapping his hands anxiously against the side of his thighs. The importance of the spaceship's safety was not lost on any of them, since they would be left with no way off the planet and no chance of survival if the ship had somehow sustained damages so heavy that it couldn't be repaired on time. Once the diagnostics were complete, the panel flashed green and Zebediah brought his pacing to an instant halt.

"Diagnostic checks completed, SLR-Titanic still at 99.8% integrity. No damage detected."

"Yes!" Tom screamed and pumped the air in excitement. "I knew I didn't damage it. I mean, come on, I'm Tom Tompson, did y'all really think there was a chance I'd screw something up so bad? I mean, sure if it'd been Tank or Scar then we would all probably be screwed."

"You mind taking a couple steps closer and saying that straight to my face?" Tank grunted.

"Yes, sir, as a matter of fact, I do mind," Tom responded and flipped the middle finger at Tank once more. "Now that I know I haven't just doomed us all, I think I'll go take a decon shower, and administer a dose of the HSS-Serum."

"Uh, I'll come too," Artemis said quickly, then stared straight at the ground. "You know...to err...uhh...to help with the serum. It can be really painful if you miss the vein and all, you know?"

"Good idea," Tom smiled. "Uh, yeah, she'll help."

"Would ye two lovebirds just stop being so embarrassing and go have your messy, carnal shower and whatnot," Scar hissed. "And try to tone down the loud high-pitched noises this time...I hear anything I don't want to hear, I'll jam an arrow down my ears."

Tom scratched the back of his head. "Speaking of arrows, think we could borrow the pulsehead arrow again?"

"You mean the arrow that vibrates?" Scar asked.

"Jesus Christ, you guys used an arrow?" Zebediah asked, a deeply bothered expression on his face.

"See, it's not as disturbing as it sounds," Tom explained. "Instead of regular sharp arrowheads, the pulsehead just has this round head...that pulses. Or vibrates. You ask me, I think it's weird that Scar even has vibrating arrows, I mean, come on, that's just nasty."

"Stop talking and just go take your shower," Zebediah groaned, deciding he had heard far more than enough information about Tom and Artemis's deeply terrifying, potentially nightmare-inducing coital activities. He had enough apocalyptic thoughts on his mind as it was.

Tom headed off in the direction of the section of the warehouse where Zebediah had placed decontamination showers, Artemis's hands in his, the two of them giggling as they half-walked/half-jumped away.

Tank grunted and dropped to the ground with a loud thud, rummaging into his pockets and pulling out a pack of cigarettes and a lighter, placing one cigarette in his mouth and lighting it before returning the pack and the lighter to his pocket. "Well, ship's not broken and we managed to all make it out of that scary mess. What's next then? Vacation for a couple hours?"

"Find something to eat," Zebediah answered. "Take a shower if you feel like it. Polish your weapons, reload, refuel, whatever you need to do. In one hour, we move out again."

Scar frowned. "We're headed out?"

Zebediah nodded. "We still haven't gotten our hands on the andrium and without andrium as a fuel source, the ship's pretty much just one oversized, glamorous container. It's not going to rise twenty feet into the air, let alone get into orbit without the andrium. We gotta acquire the fuel, run a few more diagnostics, see how the Titanic performs in action, and then we get as many people as we can off the planet."

"You want us to go back to Xtrium?" Vic asked, a confused look on his face. "The same abandoned military facility that's pretty much a nest for those walking dead things? Look, I love blasting zombie guts as much as the next guy but I ain't about to head back to Xtrium after all that's just happened."

"And I understand that," Zebediah said. "It's fine. Anyone who doesn't want to head to Xtrium can stay back here at the warehouse or do whatever, I'm not giving orders or anything."

"Nah, c'mon, don't do that," Vic groaned.

Zebediah frowned. "Do what?"

"What you're doing right now," Vic responded. "The whole 'it's fine if you don't want to put your life on the line for this mission anymore, I'm more than willing to go out there on my own. Thanks for everything you've done so far' speech."

"I wasn't going there."

"So where were you going?"

Zebediah shrugged. "Uh, I don't know. I guess I was just going to say it's fine if you didn't want to put your life at risk so soon after what just happened and I can't exactly force you to do something you don't want to, but I am grateful for your help so far...and uhh...yes, I am willing to go out there on my own."

Scar and Vic groaned in unison, while Tank chuckled.

"What?" Zebediah asked. "What's wrong with what I said?"

"That's guilt-tripping, my dude," Tank answered and chuckled. "Pretty effective, if I might add. Was about to agree with Vic here and say there's no way in hell I'm heading back out there but see, now I can't agree with Vic without feeling like a royal asshole so yeah, whenever you're ready to ride out, I'm ready."

Vic sighed. "Fine, whatever. I'll ride out too."

"You guys sure?" Zebediah smiled sheepishly. "I mean, like I said, it's totally, totally fine if you don't want to—,"

"Oh, bug off," Scar muttered and flipped the middle finger at him before grinning. "I think I'll take a shower then grab some grub to eat. Then we can go on another one of Zee Zee's trademark suicide missions."

"You're a darling," Zebediah grinned.

Zebediah performed a bunch of manual diagnostic checks on the ship just for absolute certainty that nothing was damaged while the others took showers or replenished their energy with a meal—although Tank seemed to have religiously believed he could replenish his energy with cigarettes since all he did for the one hour the others got ready was smoke. When everyone finally gathered outside the spaceship, he grunted and rose to his feet, coughing slightly as he rose.

"Ah, bloody lungs hurt," he complained.

"Smoke a few more sticks, maybe they'll hurt less," Vic joked.

Zebediah climbed out of the spaceship, put it back in cloaked mode and looked at the others, groaning in his mind when he saw Tom whisper something into Artemis's ear, to which she responded with a rather odd giggle, running a hand down his chest while she laughed. When they started drawing closer to each other, leaning forward for a kiss, Zebediah cleared his throat extremely loudly. "Looks like we're all set. Everyone understands what we're doing, right?"

"Barge into a military facility turned zombie nest to retrieve some high-power, high-efficient fuel source that's been used to power up weapons of mass destruction in the past," Tank said. "Yup, we understand."

"The andrium is the only thing that can power up the Solar Titanic," Zebediah said. "If we can't get our hands on some andrium then we're not getting off this planet and if we don't get off this planet, we'll all be dead in less than two weeks. So yeah, it's very, very important that we get as many Andromedans as we can off the planet."

"And we need to be careful while moving the andrium," Tom added. "Let's just say it's pretty sensitive so you know...if it, uh, acts up or anything...it'll be extremely lethal. I'm talking the sort of lethal where there isn't even a trace of you left behind. So that means no smoking around the andrium."

Tank growled.

"Also goes without saying that you should probably not engage in romantic or coital activities around the andrium," Scar added, narrowing her eyes at Tom and Artemis. "If I die because you lot can't keep it in your pants, I'll kill you."

"I'm with Scar on that one," Zebediah grinned then slung his rifle across his shoulder and picked up his backpack, slinging it across his back. "We'll take the speedtruck. Vic takes the wheels this time."

They headed in the direction of the speedtruck which was parked in the darker corners of the warehouse—areas where Zebediah hadn't bothered to place light strips or fluorescent bulbs—alongside other vehicles. There was an old rickety Sedan parked on the left of the speed truck with a bloodstained convertible with a cracked windshield parked on the right of it. Next to the convertible, five bikes were parked—and it would have been sex if Zebediah hadn't had to sacrifice his bike to lure the zombies away from him earlier. There was supposed to be a second truck, one the others had used to get to Xtrium before but Zebediah was certain they must have ditched the truck at some point after being overwhelmed by zombies, but he wasn't too bothered by it—there were lots of abandoned vehicles on the streets that he could freely claim, after all, none of the vehicles parked in the warehouse had truly belonged to him.

Vic climbed into the driver's seat and Zebediah sat next to him in the passenger's seat while Scar, Tom, and Artemis took the seats in the back with Scar positioning herself between Tom and Artemis so they wouldn't be able to engage in anything that'd make everyone else uncomfortable, and Tank sat in the back of the truck, pulling out a stick of cigarette the moment he'd made himself comfortable in the back. Once they were out of the warehouse, Zebediah climbed out of the truck and made sure the doors were locked before hurrying back into the truck after a group of zombies emerged from just beside the warehouse, Vic bringing his foot down hard on the pedal as soon as Zebediah was comfortably seated, rapidly putting some distance between them and the warehouse.

The first seven minutes of the drive were largely quiet, with the only sounds being the hushed whispering coming from Tom and Artemis in the back seat and Scar's irritated groans every couple of seconds, and once there was a loud yelp from Tom after Scar had punched him hard in the stomach when he'd tried to stretch across her to kiss Artemis, with Vic and Zebediah chuckling at the sound of Tom's pain. A few minutes later, Tank started to drum in the back of the truck, singing loudly enough that those seated inside the car could clearly make out his horrible, almost torturous rendition of a song from the 90s, his singing gradually getting louder and louder until Tom was eventually forced to stick his head out the window and yell for Tank to be quiet, to which Tank responded exactly as Zebediah had imagined he would—with louder singing.

"Let him keep it up," Vic said and smiled. "A sound that terrible, it'll keep all the crazies away from us. He's clearing us a path to Xtrium with a voice like that."

"It ain't that bad, to be fair," Scar shrugged. "I mean, my dead nana sounded a lot better than that but it ain't bad. I've heard worse."

"I refuse to believe there's a worse sound than that," Tom said.

"Trust me, there is," Scar responded. "Stepped on my cat accidentally once. Sound she made was the stuff of my nightmares for the next couple of weeks after. Scary stuff, really."

"And now you're going to have to go through all of that again," Tom joked.

The rest of the drive to Xtrium was rather uneventful and even though Zebediah had hoped for exactly that, he couldn't help but feel deeply bothered by how quiet and peaceful the drive had been...it had been far too peaceful. The only zombies they spotted were ones who'd had their legs blasted off and were attempting to drag themselves across the ground with their hands in search of their next meal, and while Zebediah hadn't said anything in the car so he wouldn't come off as too much of a pessimist, he kept his guard up when they arrived at Xtrium and all got down from the truck, maintaining a tight grip on his rifle while scanning the facility for any signs of trouble.

Tank must have noticed the look on Zebediah's face since he moved towards him and grunted. "No birds."

Zebediah frowned at him. "What?"

Tank pointed upwards. "Kept me eyes on the sky when we were coming here. Too quiet, and no birds flying over. My experience, means something must have gone on around here, something that's scared 'em birdies away. We might be walking into a horrible death trap here, boss."

Zebediah sighed and looked around at the group, all of the others with fierce looks on their faces. "Everyone, keep your guards up. Something feels off about this, so just stay at alert. You know the rules: if it's not one of us and if it walks funny, shoot it. Just try not to shoot the andrium containers, that'd be lights out for every single one of us."

"Got it," Tank grunted, and was about to light another cigarette but Scar moved quickly, snatched the cigarette from him, crushed it in her palm and tossed it aside. When Tank tried to get another, she stole the entire pack off him and hurled it a great distance away.

"No smoking around a fuel source that could disintegrate us all," she said.

"Oh, fuck off," Tank growled.

After looking around the facility's compound for signs of trouble, Zebediah led the others to the main entrance which was wide open, as he'd expected considering the place had long since been abandoned. Beyond the entrance, a pile of headless zombie bodies awaited them, with Zebediah showing extra care in navigating around the bodies, while scrunching up his nose in an attempt to block out the rather putrid odor that filled the air around them, his eyes stinging as a result of the foul stench.

Tom made a retching sound as he accidentally stepped on one of the bodies, his foot sinking straight through with a squishing sound and when he pulled his foot out, there was blood and yellow goo on his shoe and the lower part of his denim trousers. Tank grunted and kicked a body aside, chuckling at the squishing sound the body made when it hit the wall.

"Sick," Tom groaned.

"This isn't right," Vic murmured, moving slowly. They ventured deeper into the facility, so deep that the light that was flooding in through the entrance could no longer reach them, darkness starting to engulf them as they progressed. Once it got so dark that they could barely make out anything, they all switched on the flashlights attached to their weapons, aiming it around so they could see their surroundings and be sure they weren't headed into another zombie nest. "This isn't right," Vic murmured again. "I think we should turn around."

Zebediah frowned in his direction. "Do you see something? Is something wrong?"

"Too many of them are dead," Vic answered.

"In what world is that a bad thing?" Tank queried. "Dead zombies translates to less stress for us and less of a chance that we get our throats ripped out by them rotten crazies. Quit complaining, lad."

Vic turned around, a fearful expression on his face. "Tank, when we were here earlier, did you see this many dead zombies laying around?"

Tank frowned as he pondered, then his eyes widened with realization. "Someone else has been here. Someone else did all of this, took out the zombies that were nested here. It's why there's no birds, there must have been incredible chaos here while we were dealing with our situation."

Zebediah halted. "One person couldn't have left behind all of these bodies."

"And why take out this many zombies then just bail?" Tom queried, gently stepping around one of the bodies. "Everything else looks the same as it was when we were here earlier. Who the hell's going around killing these things and just leaving without taking anything?"

"Unless they haven't left," Artemis murmured.

"We need to get the hell out of here right now," Zebediah's voice was panicked. "It's a trap. Someone set this trap for us."

They turned around on their heels instantly, moving at a rapid pace back in the direction from which they'd come but they hadn't covered a lot of distance when the facility's lights all suddenly came on, the sudden increase in brightness causing all of them to shut their eyes instinctively, groaning at the slight ache of their eyes in reaction to the light. Zebediah cracked his eyes open slightly and blinked repeatedly as he tried to force them to adjust to the incredibly bright lights of the facility, but once they did adjust, he immediately wished they hadn't since he hadn't expected to find himself staring at a horde of men donning camo uniforms and military-grade bulletproof vests, all of them wielding rifles with their sights trained on Zebediah and the rest of the group, red dots appearing all over Zebediah's body. Zebediah aimed his weapon at one of the soldiers but he knew even if he took his shot, he'd be pumped full of bullets before he could even take in a breath of oxygen.

"Uhm, Zee Zee, I thought you said this military facility was abandoned?" Tom said. "Cause right now, it looks to me like it was still being used by the military and err, they've got quite a lot of guns aimed at us now."

"It was abandoned," Zebediah responded, his eyes darting from left to right as he studied the soldiers that had surrounded them. "These soldiers only just arrived here at Xtrium."

"Right you are, Mr. Zebediah Ezekial," a voice said and a soldier with white hair, white beards and ghostly gray eyes stepped forward, the only soldier in there who wasn't donning a bulletproof vest. His skin was rough in patches, clearly worn by age and battle, and he had this cold look to his gray eyes. "We weren't always here. But you see, after looking through the feed from this facility and discovering that a group of survivors had attempted to break in to search for a material capable of powering incredible weapons of mass destruction, we sort of decided we had to check it out. Helps that your men lured away quite a handful of the damn crazies, gave my boys and I much less cleaning up to do."

"Who the hell are you?" Tank grunted.

"General Alistair Prometheus," the soldier answered in his gruff voice, a momentary glint in his eyes. "Andromedan Planetary Military. And I'm afraid we're going to have to take you and your friends in for questioning."

Zebediah snorted. "Questioning? For what? We've committed no crimes."

"Need I remind you that you're currently standing inside of a military facility that's a restricted area for the civilian populace of this planet?" Prometheus asked. "It's not every day that a group of civilians go off in search of a nuclear power source as dangerous as andrium."

"We need the andrium for something," Vic explained. "We're not trying to set off a nuclear explosion or anything of the sort. We just need it to power up something, something that could help the Andromedans survive this virus."

Prometheus smiled. "I assume you're talking about the spacecraft being stored in your cozy little warehouse?"

Zebediah felt his heart sink to the depths of his stomach, a sudden lightheaded sensation washing over him. Seconds that felt like eternity passed as his mind went blank, with absolutely no idea what to say next. When he finally did speak, his voice was hoarse. "You got into the warehouse?"

"Right after we detected activity here in this facility, scouts reported there'd been an explosion not too far out from here. Had a squadron head over there, watching the warehouse that you boys went into. Soon as you left, they broke in, had a look around. Reported the discovery of one very massive spacecraft, which is kinda surprising since it's illegal to own a spacecraft without authorization."

"I built it," Zebediah growled.

"Oh, trust me, we're certain you did," Prometheus said. "Never seen a spacecraft like that my whole life and I've been around my fair share of spaceships and space shuttles. What I'm wondering is how you managed to build something like that right under our noses, and what you're planning to do with it."

"If there's so much as a single scratch on that ship, I'll kill you," Zebediah growled. "I don't care what happens to me after, but if that ship gets damaged, I'll kill every single one of you."

"Oh, we're not going to damage the ship at all," Prometheus smiled. "We're just going to be taking it off your hands."

"Over my dead body." Zebediah growled.

Zebediah took a step towards Prometheus but as soon as he did, there was a loud BANG! as one of the soldiers fired a shot from his weapon, the bullet shooting straight through Tom's shoulder, with Tom letting out an agonized yell and dropping to his knees, one hand clutching the spot where he'd just been shot, blood seeping out of the wound at an alarming rate.

"Tom!" Artemis screamed and had only taken a step towards him when a bullet hit the ground, missing her foot by a mere inch, causing her to stop dead in her tracks, her hands trembling.

"I don't think you understand us, Mr. Ezekial," Prometheus said, an evil glint in his eyes. "You will do exactly as I say, or I'm afraid we will have to inflict grossly mindblowing amounts of agony on your little posse. And make no mistake, we have no qualms against killing every single one of you. Do you understand me?"

Tank turned the safety on his gun off, the weapon trained right at Prometheus's head. "I'll blow the brains right out of this son of a bitch, just say the word, Zee Zee," Tank grunted.

Zebediah bit his lips, weighing the severity of the situation they were currently in. Even if Tank killed Prometheus, they would instantly be executed by the other soldiers who'd surrounded them. There was no way to walk out of this facility alive...not unless they complied.

"Lower your gun, Tank," Zebediah ordered.

Tank frowned at him. "Uh, what? What the hell?"

"We can't fight our way out of this one," Zebediah said and lowered his weapon. He looked into Prometheus's cold eyes, wearing a defeated expression on his face. "I surrender. You can have the ship. You've got us, we're smoked."

Prometheus smiled. "I'm pleased you—,"

Tom moved with speed, running into Artemis and Scar, pushing them behind cover, while Zebediah, Tank, and Vic all rushed for cover. Before the soldiers could open fire, there was a hissing sound and smoke poured out of cannisters that Tom had dropped onto the ground before rushing for cover, clogging the air and preventing the soldiers from seeing them.

The soldiers made coughing sounds and fired blindly but ceased fire after Prometheus barked at them. Zebediah broke into a sprint, a hand shielding his nose as he ran, hurried footsteps coming from behind him and ahead of him, though he couldn't make out who the footsteps belonged to through all of this smoke. Just when the entrance came into visibility and a smile of relief had spread across his face, he felt crippling pain ripple throughout his body as a bullet went straight through his knee, sending him dropping to the ground immediately, a scream escaping his mouth.

Firm hands grabbed him on either side and lifted him up. "Come on, Zee Zee," it was Artemis. "I've got you."

"No," Zebediah said and dropped back to the ground, sitting and resting his back against the wall, his face soaked in sweat with his eyes watery. "Go. Leave me here. They won't do anything to me."

"Are you out of your mind?!" Artemis exclaimed. "I'm not leaving you."

"Artemis, go!" Zebediah yelled. "Get out of here."

"Zee Zee."

"Artemis, go. Please," Zebediah said and shifted his wounded knee, groaning in pain as he did. "The rest of you get out of here. They won't hurt me, ship's useless to them without me."

"What the hell do we do without you?!"

"Find the andrium," Zebediah smiled. Footsteps came from just behind them, and Zebediah heard the distinct voice of Prometheus, barking at the other soldiers as they searched for them. Zebediah looked into Artemis's eyes. "Go."

A tear rolled down Artemis's face, then she turned around on her heels and sprinted off, the soldiers arriving where Zebediah was moments after Artemis had gotten out of the facility. Prometheus walked towards Zebediah, grabbed him by the throat and lifted him up with ease.

"Where are they?!" Prometheus growled.

"Beats me," Zebediah chuckled. "But seeing as it's just you and me now, how's about we talk this through like adults and try to reach an agreement that's satisfactory for the both of us."

"Do we go in pursuit of the others?" a soldier asked.

Prometheus shook his head. "Nah, let them go. He's the one we need, he's the brains behind that spacecraft. Plus, without him, those morons aren't going to get very far."

"What exactly do you want with my ship?"

"What do you think?" Prometheus hissed, bringing his face so close that Zebediah could feel the heat of his breath. "You're going to tell us exactly how to work that plane and then we're going to get the hell of his planet."

"And if I choose to be somewhat uncooperative?"

Prometheus smashed a fist into Zebediah's stomach, knocking the wind right out of him before shoving him to the ground. "You're going to help us survive this damn thing, or I'm going to kill you."

Chapter Four

ZEBEDIAH'S DECISION to let the others escape while he surrendered himself over to Prometheus's soldiers was one he came to greatly regret over the next four days, when he truly realized the harsh, sadistic extent to which Prometheus was willing to go to motivate Zebediah to power up the Solar Titanic for the military's benefit. Their plan was simple: use the ship to get the soldiers off planet, then find a different planet to colonize and adopt as a new home, a plan far more violent than Zebediah's plan which was to simply seek shelter on a different planet. For four days, Zebediah had told Prometheus that the ship was far from complete and that he still had a lot of work to do before it was ready to head into space but it was clear now that Prometheus was starting to get tired of Zebediah's excuses since when he came today, it had been with other soldiers, who used tasers on Zebediah every time he gave an unacceptable answer.

When Zebediah's answer didn't change, Prometheus called the soldiers off and then stormed off angrily, leaving Zebediah to stare up at his spaceship, which had been moved from the warehouse by the military to whichever facility he was currently being held in. He sighed and headed towards the spaceship, dropping to the ground next to hit, his back leaning against the side of the ship. He wiped the sweat off his face with the sleeves of his shirt, a shirt that now had a terrible sweaty odor seeing as he'd been in it for four consecutive days, and hadn't even been allowed to take a decontamination shower. He still received dosages of the serum, but the privilege of cleaning himself up wasn't one he'd been given by the planetary military.

It was only a matter of time till Prometheus realized that Zebediah was only holding out, stalling so his friends could get what they needed to power the ship up and then come find him. It was only a matter of time till he realized that Zebediah had been creating a mental map of the entire facility since he'd been dragged in here, and that Zebediah was figuring out a way to hack into the facility's security system using the ship's supercomputers and if he'd paid far more attention in computer class, he would no doubt have accessed the security systems by now, but for now, it would be a loop of trial and error until he somehow figured it out.

After resting by the side of the ship for about half an hour, Zebediah rose onto his feet and headed into the ship, sitting by the computers which instantly recognized him and powered up the moment he took his seat. It was time for him to get back to orchestrating his great escape. Once he was connected to the security systems, he'd have access to all of the surveillance within the facility so he could figure out the least risky way out of the facility. Not to mention, with access to the security systems, he could probably turn the facility's security measures against the soldiers to make his escape far easier. He just had to figure all of this out first, and quickly. He'd been here four days, that meant they had even less time to get as many people as they could off the planet.

Zebediah got so engrossed in his attempt to gain access into the building's security that he forgot to look out to check when Prometheus or some of his soldiers were coming to keep up with his progress. It was only when he heard voices just outside the ship that he hastily rose off the chair, turned the computers off and spun around just as Prometheus came into visibility, flanked by two gruff-looking soldiers, with one blond, short, timid-looking man who had to be in his mid-twenties standing behind them. Prometheus and the other soldiers were in military uniform, but the blond man donned a white T-shirt atop black trousers and a pair of white sneakers, with fingerless gloves worn on either hand.

"Any progress, Big Brains?" Prometheus queried.

Zebediah cleared his throat. "Uh, a little. Just ran diagnostic checks on the neutranium filters and they seem to be fully fixed right now. Just gotta check out a couple more things, make sure everything's a hundred percent ready because flying this thing at any less than that would be suicidal. Moronium pipes are still damaged, I'll get around to fixing that soon."

The man in the white T-shirt cleared his throat. "Moronium pipes?"

Zebediah nodded. "Uh-uh, yeah yeah. Really important pipes, they're necessary for uh...really technical stuff that I don't want to get into since it'll take up too much time and as General Prometheus here has made known on multiple occasions, time isn't something that's on my side."

"Ah, I see," the man said, his eyes meeting Zebediah's for a split second before he pulled them away.

"Zebediah Ezekial, this is Ryan," Prometheus said, gesturing towards the man in white. "He's an engineer who's worked for me for quite some time now, and seeing as you seem to be having difficulties getting this baby up and running, I've asked him to lend you a hand. After all, two heads are better than one, right?"

"Not if one of them's yours," Zebediah muttered.

Prometheus frowned. "What's that?"

"Nothing," Zebediah answered quickly. "Nothing at all."

"Right," Prometheus continued. "Anyways, Ryan's with you now and since I've run out of patience, you now have twenty-four hours to get this ship running or I just might get really temperamental and say, I don't know, kill one of you. Maybe even the two of you."

"Won't be necessary, I assure you," Zebediah forced a smile.

"Just get it running," Prometheus hissed then turned around and headed off the ship with the other soldiers, leaving Ryan behind with Zebediah, the two of them staring awkwardly in silence before the silence was finally broken by Ryan.

"Moronium isn't an actual thing," Ryan said calmly, casting a glance around the ship, looking somewhat impressed by it. "That means you really haven't been trying to fix this, have you?"

"If you want to fix something, it's gotta be broken first, don't it?" Zebediah snorted.

"So the ship's in optimal condition?" Ryan asked.

"Duh."

"Why would you tell me that? Not worried I'm going to let Prometheus know that you're lying to him, and probably buying time for some sinister plan you're orchestrating? Maybe you're waiting for your friends to come break you out?"

"You knew moronium wasn't a real thing when I said it," Zebediah replied. "You could have brought my ruse crashing down there and then, but you didn't and I'm guessing that's because you're not much of a fan of his either. So no, I don't think you're going to let him know I'm lying...hell, I even believe you're going to help me get the hell out of this place."

"Why would I do that?"

"Because you're here against your will too," Zebediah answered, making eye contact with Ryan again, taking note of the sadness in his eyes. "Explains why he'd threaten to kill you too."

Ryan folded his arms. "I'm going to save you a lot of energy by telling you this right now: it's impossible to break out of this facility. Security measures here are insane and there's soldiers on patrol round the clock. If you're seen where you shouldn't be, they have instructions to fire on sight."

"What if I could gain remote access to the security system?" Zebediah asked with a grin on his face. "I assume it'd be easy to bypass the facility's security if we're in control of it?"

Ryan snorted. "You're not going to gain remote access to the facility's security system. There's incredibly powerful firewalls set up to prevent malicious attacks and I know because some of them are based on my code. To get in, you'd need a really powerful computer and all of the computers are down in level 3, and as I'm sure you'd know, we don't have the authorization to just waltz in there."

Zebediah powered up the computers again then looked at Ryan. "Will this be good enough?"

"Holy," Ryan murmured, staring in awe at the computers. "How the hell did you get these computers in here?"

"Used to have a friend way back who knew his way around computers and whatnot," Zebediah answered, his face and voice falling as he spoke. "He helped out a lot with the construction of the ship. He was part of the crew. And then one day, we went in search of materials for the ship, got overwhelmed by a horde of the crazies and he laid down his life to buy the rest of us enough time to get away. If he were here right now, this facility would be burning down to the ground already."

"Yeah, yeah, whatever, sorry about that," Ryan said and quickly sat by the computer, his face lighting up like that of an excited child as he immediately went to work, his fingers clicking away at the keyboard. "This should only take about thirty minutes. One hour, tops."

Zebediah snorted. "That's impossible, buddy. I've been doing this for days."

"Majored as a computer software engineer, got a second degree in data science as well as a doctorate. Wrote my first malware when I was ten, hacked into my school's systems to give every student perfect grades when I was twelve, and every now and then, when I need to research on something, I just access restricted databases. Trust me, you and I are not the same."

"Well, I built a functioning aircraft when I was twelve," Zebediah muttered.

"What'd you do when you were ten?" Ryan asked.

"Piss off."

There was silence between the both of them for well over forty minutes as Zebediah simply paced around while Ryan attempted to gain access to the facility's security, with forty-six minutes going by before he finally let out an excited yell and punched the air. Zebediah rushed towards him and stared at the screens which displayed live footage from all of the surveillance cameras within the facility, with Zebediah's mind starting to calculate various ways by which he could get out of the facility safely. Finally, he noticed something on the surveillance that caught his attention.

"Whoa, what's that?" he asked and tapped his finger against the screen, at footage of a dimly lit room filled pods, and glass boxes—no, cages—that seemed to be contain people.

Ryan looked at Zebediah, a sad look in his eyes. "You don't know about it?"

Zebediah frowned. "Know what?"

"They're all infected," Ryan answered, staring at the live footage. "There's a lab here, they try to research the infection, to try to develop something stronger than the HSS-Serum. Or at least, that's how it started. It's gotten sick and twisted recently, and now they're injecting people with the disease or virus or whatever the fuck it is, as part of their testing. The zombies in those pods, in the cages, that's the result of their testing."

Zebediah's heart sunk. "They're destroying people's lives, they're turning people to those things. Why isn't anyone doing anything about this?"

"Because the people who try to stop it end up in those cages too," Ryan said and looked away, clenching his fists firmly. "Better to get with the program than be a victim of it."

"Once Prometheus finds out there isn't anything to fix in this ship, once I've outlived my usefulness to him, I'm going to end up in one of those pods or cages," Zebediah said. "This is sick."

"Yeah, it is," Ryan agreed, his tone deeply sad. He cleared his throat, and then added, "Now you know why I chose not to let him know you were trolling with the whole moronium bit."

"We have to stop Prometheus," Zebediah said fiercely. "And then we get the hell out of this place."

"Got any plans?"

"Depends."

"On what?"

"Is there any andrium in this facility?" Zebediah asked, squinting at the live feeds from the surveillance cameras, trying to find a room that housed andrium fuel containers. He had to be sure there was andrium here.

"Are you kidding?" Ryan asked and snorted. "Entire facility is powered up by the thing."

Zebediah smiled. "Then yeah, I have a plan. But I'm going to need to send out a message to a couple friends first."

***

Ryan had long since drifted off to sleep in one of the seats aboard the ship which he'd adjusted for peak comfortability, his loud, incessant snoring that was reminiscent of the sound of a tractor the only thing that kept Zebediah awake as he kept his eyes trained on the computer screen, monitoring the facility's live surveillance feed. If his message had been delivered, and received by Tank and the others then sleep wasn't something he could do right now—he needed to be awake for what was about to come, so really, he was glad about Ryan's snoring.

An hour passed without anything interesting happening, and with the time now being three hours past midnight, Zebediah was starting to seriously doubt whether the others had gotten the message and even if they had, maybe they'd just decided they weren't willing to risk everything by charging into a fully active military facility. He was just about to move away from the computers to the seat next to Ryan so he could get some shuteye when he noticed a truck coming to a stop just outside the facility's gates, the guards positioned there moving towards the truck.

There were flashes, no doubt from guns being fired and all four guards dropped to the ground, and a smile crept onto Zebediah's face when Tank stared straight at the camera and waved in greeting.

"Ryan!" Zebediah yelled.

Ryan woke with a gasp, rolling out of the seat immediately before clumsily rising to his feet, rubbing his eyes as he moved towards Zebediah. "What's going on?" he asked groggily.

"They're here," Zebediah grinned. "Set off the alarms on levels 5 and 6. And get those gates open."

"Level 6?" Ryan asked. "That's where the zombie research lab is. Or zombie dungeon, whatever the hell it's supposed to be."

"Oh, trust me, I'm well aware that's where it is," Zebediah said, his voice steely. "I need to get as many soldiers as possible down to level 6, so there's very few we have to deal with to get the andrium being stored in level 3."

"Prometheus will come here once the alarms go off," Ryan warned. "He'll want to make sure that we're not the cause of the alarms, and trust me, he won't come alone."

"I'm counting on it," Zebediah grinned. "Set off the alarms now. And get those gates open."

Ryan nodded and sat by the computers, clicking away as he accessed the alarm systems. A couple of seconds passed and then, Zebediah picked up on the distant sound of alarms blaring, the surveillance feed showing the lights on levels 5 and 6 now flashing red. Ryan hit a key, and Zebediah watched as the facility's gates slid open, the truck which had Tom at the wheel driving into the facility, while Tank looked at the camera and held up a hand.

Five fingers. Five minutes. Five minutes till they were here to get Zebediah and the ship out of here.

"Get ready," Zebediah said to Ryan. "We've got five minutes."

"Five minutes till what?"

Zebediah got up and moved towards a silvery chest, inputting a couple of digits before the chest opened up slightly, a hissing sound coming from it. Zebediah opened it up completely and pulled out a pistol, tossing it to Ryan who fumbled the catch and had to bend to get the gun from the ground. Zebediah pulled out two more pistols, and a small bag filled with grenades, slinging the bag across his shoulder.

"Five minutes till all hell breaks loose," he answered, then switched the safety on the guns off.

Chapter Five

ONCE ENOUGH SOLDIERS had gathered on level 6, Ryan locked down the level, trapping them in there before remote accessing the pods and cages and opening them up, freeing the zombies that had been trapped within, giving the soldiers down there something that would keep them easy. The same was done to level five, with the level being locked down once enough soldiers had reported to investigate the alarm, although there were no zombies there to unleash on them—not yet, at least. Zebediah, on the other hand, stood next to the spaceship, waiting for Prometheus and his soldiers to pop up, but five minutes passed without any sign of them, then, without warning, the doors were blasted open and Tank strutted in, a smile of satisfaction on his face; Tom and Artemis walked in just after him, beaming smiles on their faces.

"Zee Zee!" Artemis yelled excitedly. "We got the message!"

"Good," Zebediah said then frowned. "Vic and Scar, where are they?"

"Acquiring the andrium," Tank answered, and tossed a rifle to Zebediah who caught it perfectly, then slung the rifle across his back. "Heard you got shot, how's the leg?"

Zebediah shrugged. "They were kind enough to patch me up after shooting me, so yeah, it's all good now. Stings like a bitch but at least I can walk on it, so I suppose that's good. Real kind of them."

"Yeah, real mighty kind," Tank grunted, and started to reload his gun. "Paid a couple of them back on the way in here by sending 'em to meet their makers. They shoot one of us, I shoot all of them."

"Well, looks like there's a bunch more for you to shoot," Zebediah said, as a group of soldiers appeared in the hall just beyond where the doors had previously been, all of them armed with rifles. Zebediah acted quickly, opening fire at them, managing to land shots at two of them, forcing the others to retreat for cover. He dipped his hand into his bag, brought two grenades out, removed the pins from them and threw them forward, the grenades landing just where the soldiers had chosen to take cover.

"Shit, grenade!" a soldier yelled, and they started to scramble away from the grenade but didn't make it very far before it detonated, the blast from the explosion sending the soldiers flying through the air, pieces of shrapnel lodging themselves painfully in the soldiers. The blast from the grenade had filled the hallway with smoke, making it impossible for them to make out anything in there, which was exactly why none of them saw the shot coming. There was the loud BANG! of a gunshot and the sound of a bullet shooting through flesh as Tank let out a loud growl and looked at the spot on his arm where the bullet had gone straight through, a relatively unconcerned look on his face.

He cursed under his breath, growled again and fired into the hallway, into the smoke, firing despite not knowing who his targets were. Once he'd emptied his weapon's ammo, he took a couple of deep breaths and stared into the hallway, as if waiting to see if someone else would try to shoot at him. When no shot came, he lowered his gun and grunted. "Now I've gotta deal with this weird burning itch," he pressed a finger against the bullet wound, winced slightly then ripped his tank top off and tied it firmly around the wound to stop the bleeding. Zebediah had seen Tank topless before, but he still couldn't help but be mindblown by his incredible physique, with his bulging biceps, toned pecks and firm-looking six packs—the physical features that had earned him his nickname.

"There's a first aid kit on the ship," Zebediah said. "You could have just...you know...asked. You didn't have to...you know...do the whole ripping off your shirt to prove you're incredibly built thing."

Tank grinned. "There's a lot of things I don't have to but if I'm gonna look cool and badass doing it then you bet your sweet ass I'll be doing it. Now let's go hunt down some annoying military men."

"We gotta stay here, with the ship," Tom said. "We need to wait for Vic and Scar to get back to us with the andrium."

As if it'd been rehearsed and perfectly timed, Vic and Scar emerged from the smoke-clogged hallway, both bloodstained and covered in dirt and soot, jointly pushing a massive container with wheels. As soon as they came into visibility, Tank hurried towards them and lent his assistance, wheeling the container in before letting go, Vic and Scar bending over and taking deep breaths.

"Well, there's your andrium," Vic groaned and wiped sweat off his face with his sleeves. "You probably should have mentioned in your message that these sons of bitches have some way of controlling the zombies and using them like lapdogs. It was hell having to deal with so many crazies."

Zebediah frowned. "What the hell are you talking about?"

Ryan rushed out of the ship that instant with a frantic expression on his face. "I'm being overridden, and there's something you should know. Prometheus, he's headed here and he's not alone."

"How many soldiers?" Tom asked.

"That's the thing," Ryan responded, "he's not coming with soldiers. He's coming with zombies. A fuck ton of zombies, he's controlling them somehow."

"Get the andrium onto the ship now," Zebediah said, looking at Tank and the others. "We need to get the hell out of this place right fucking now." He looked to Ryan. "Try to slow him down as much as you can, buy us enough time to load the andrium onto the ship."

"I don't have that much control anymore but sure, I'll try to slow him down," Ryan said. "Just hurry up, we don't have a lot of time left."

Scar and Artemis positioned themselves in front of the entrance, weapons aimed into the hallway, readying themselves to fire at any zombie or soldier who appeared there, while Tank opened up the massive container and lifted one andrium fuel container with ease, hurrying towards the ship with it while Tom, Vic, and Zebediah lifted more containers, albeit with a lot of struggle considering none of them was made entirely of muscle like Tank.

They'd moved eight containers onto the ship when Scar and Artemis started to fire, signifying that threats had arrived. Despite feeling the strong urge to go provide assistance, Zebediah reminded himself that they had to secure the andrium first since this was their only way off the planet, and considering they'd fired at a handful of soldiers and unleashed zombies on more, they were definitely going to have to leave the planet if they were to stand a chance of surviving. Zebediah, Tank, Vic, and Tom continued to haul the andrium containers aboard the ship with Ryan also joining to make it much faster, while Scar and Artemis tried to keep the zombies at bay.

When Scar and Artemis ran out of ammo and needed to reload, that was when all hell broke loose. It was almost as if the zombies had been deliberately allowing themselves be picked off by Scar and Artemis, biding their time until the two of them needed to reload, and the moment they both paused to reload, the zombies surged forward.

"Shit!" Artemis yelled as the both of them started to retreat, the zombies advancing at a frightening pace. She finished reloading and started opening fire with Scar joining in shortly, but the zombies had already gotten in and were moving towards the ship with incredible speed, forcing the others to hold off on moving the andrium and defending the ship from being breached instead.

When one of the zombies dropped to the ground at Zebediah's feet, he noticed the blinking red light on the back of their neck and immediately realized how Prometheus had managed to control them. They had chips on the back of their necks that somehow allowed Prometheus to control the creatures, weaponizing them. It also explained how they'd been intelligent enough to know to wait until Scar and Artemis needed to reload before charging forward—Prometheus was the mind behind the hive. The military hadn't found a way to reverse the infection, so instead they'd devised a way to weaponize the infected. These zombies had once been Andromedans like Zebediah, and now they were in a state that was neither dead nor alive, being puppeteered by the sinister General.

They'd all been so distracted by the zombie horde that none of them noticed that Prometheus had somehow gotten in undetected, and it was only when a loud gunshot rang and Zebediah was grabbed by the throat from behind that they realized it. The others all looked in the direction the gunshot had come from and were shocked to find Zebediah being held by Prometheus who wore some silvery buds in his ears that blinked red, no doubt what he was using to control the zombies who had now stopped attacking and simply stood in place, snarling and growling.

"Zee Zee!" Vic yelled.

"If any of you try anything, I will not hesitate to blow his head open," Prometheus snarled, pressing the gun against Zebediah's temple. "Lower all your fucking weapons right fucking now!"

"You're not going to kill me," Zebediah snorted. "I'm the only one who can pilot the ship."

"Won't be too hard to figure it out," Prometheus hissed. "Hard as it may be for you to believe, you're not the smartest man in the world, Zebediah. Tell your buddies here to lower their weapons or I'll put a bullet in your damn head."

"No."

Prometheus aimed his gun upwards and fired again before pressing it against Zebediah's head once more. "You think I'm fucking kidding around right now?!" Prometheus asked. "I'll do it, I swear I will. Drop all your guns right now!"

"If you're going to put a bullet in my head, do it already," Zebediah said. "Neither one of them will lower their guns, and I will not teach you how to power up the ship or how to pilot it. You might have a gun against the side of my head but you're not in a position to negotiate, buddy."

"Negotiate?" Prometheus repeated. "You think I'm trying to negotiate?"

Suddenly, one of the zombies that had gone dormant charged, straight at Artemis, lunging at her, its teeth bared and ready to sink into her flesh but Tom reacted quickly, putting himself between Artemis and the zombie, the zombie's teeth sinking into his arm instead. Tom let out a loud scream then pressed his gun against the zombie's head and fired, blasting the creature's head off.

"Tom, no," Artemis gasped, her lips quivering as she saw the blood escaping Tom's wound, but the bleeding wasn't the scary part. It was what was going to happen to him in a matter of moments—the virus had been exposed directly to his blood, it was only a matter of time till he became one of those things. Till he became one of the zombies.

"I'm going to kill you for that!" Tank growled, aiming his gun at Prometheus.

Prometheus chuckled, and tapped a finger against the bud in his left ear. "With these, they'll do everything I tell them to. You will all do exactly what I ask you to, or you'll be met with the same fate that awaits your little friend. I'm sure you all know what he'll be in less than an hour."

Zebediah stared on at Tom, who rose to his feet and winced, looking at the bite on his arms before looking into Artemis's eyes and grinning wildly. "Relax, honey, it's just a bite. I've been bitten plenty of times before, remember what you and I did in the shower?"

"Tom, this isn't funny," Artemis's voice was shaky, her eyes starting to water. "The bite, it's going to—,"

"It's fine," Tom said calmly, cutting her off. "It's fine."

"Well, isn't that just cu—," there was another gunshot, one that cut Prometheus off mid-sentence, his hold on Zebediah's throat becoming loose. Zebediah freed himself, turned around quickly and punched Prometheus's gun out of his hand, before thrusting a foot into Prometheus's stomach, knocking him to the ground. Blood was rapidly seeping through Prometheus's uniform, with the bullet having come from Ryan who stood in the ship, the gun in his hand still aimed at Prometheus although his hands were trembling already.

Zebediah aimed his gun at Prometheus, ready to end it but before he could, another of the zombies charged, at him this time, crashing into him and tackling him to the ground. Before the creature could sink its teeth into Zebediah's flesh, Tank fired, blasting the zombie's head clean off, sending blood and goo splattering onto Zebediah who made spluttering sounds and wiped the blood off his face with his sleeves. As soon as he was back on his feet, another lunged at him but he moved quickly, shooting the zombie's head off while it was in the air, the headless body dropping to the ground at his feet.

Artemis hurried forward and stood over Prometheus, firing multiple times into his head before he could command another of the zombies, smashing her foot into one of the buds right after killing and letting out a feral scream, before firing a couple more bullets into Prometheus's head. Tears rolled down her face as she sniffled, and raised the gun slightly to continue firing but froze when Zebediah placed a hand on her shoulder.

"He's dead. It's done."

"Uhm, guys?" Ryan said. "I think we might want to get the hell out of here right now cause, uh, these zombies are looking famished."

They all looked in the direction of the zombies who'd started to move again, snarling and growling as they moved. Zebediah fired at a couple of them, rapidly backing up towards the ship, dragging Artemis along with him. "Everyone, get on the ship!" Zebediah yelled. "We have to get out of here now!"

Tank, Vic, and Scar sprinted towards the ship, firing at the zombies as they moved, ceasing their gunfire once they were aboard the ship. "Tom!" Tank yelled. "Get your ass on the ship right now!"

Tom looked in their direction and smiled sadly, wiping away the blood that was now coming out of his nose, his skin looking somewhat pale already. He moved forward, but not in the direction of the ship, instead progressing towards the andrium container, his hands trembling at his sides as he walked.

"Tom, what the hell are you doing?!" Artemis yelled.

Tom lifted one of the containers, and set it down on the ground right in front of him before aiming his gun upwards and firing, the sound of the gunshot causing all of the zombies to turn their attention in his direction and away from the people aboard the spaceship.

Zebediah's eyes widened in realization. "We have to get out of here right now. He's going to blow this place up."

"What?" Artemis said. "We're not leaving him!"

Zebediah wasn't listening—he hit a button on the panel that sealed the spaceship's hatch instantly. Artemis turned to face Zebediah and without warning, slapped him across the face before reaching a hand for the button to attempt opening the ship up, but Tank grabbed her and held her back.

"Let go of me!" Artemis screamed. "He's going to die!"

"Artemis, he's been bitten," Scar said sadly, her eyes reddened. "He knows what's happening to him, he's doing this so we can get out of here. So you can survive. Opening that door isn't going to save his life."

"Let go!" Artemis screamed.

Zebediah grabbed one of the andrium containers and hurried down to a lower level of the ship, carefully fitting the container over one of the pipes that would draw fuel—all he needed was for the ship to be fueled enough to get them away from the facility. He hurried back up and towards the computers, flipping a set of switches and pushing down on a button, all of the lights on the ship coming on as he powered it up. Once the ship had powered up fully, a holographic face popped up just over the computers.

"ZEB-SLR71," he said as soon as the face popped up.

"Recognized, Zebediah Ezekial. How may I help you?"

"Titan, get us out of here," Zebediah ordered.

"No!" Artemis screamed, but the ship started to vibrate as its engines powered up, rising into the air almost immediately. "You can't do this!"

"Artemis!" Zebediah yelled angrily and turned to face her, the tears he'd been fighting back pouring out of his eyes now. "I don't want to do this, but we have to! He's doing this so we can get away from here, so we can make it off world. He's saving our lives and I'm not going to let you throw that sacrifice away by opening up that hatch, do you understand me?!"

"Tank, let her go," Vic said softly.

Tank obliged and let go of Artemis who immediately dropped to her knees, burying her face in her hands and weeping profusely. Zebediah shook his head and wiped the tears off his face, then hit another button which activated the ship's shields.

The ship shot forward with incredible speed, straight through the wall, the shields taking the damage with ridiculous ease, and they hadn't gotten very far from the facility when it exploded, the shockwave from the blast reaching them and causing the ship to tilt slightly before the AI adjusted it, the shields still holding up greatly.

Where the facility had been, there was now nothing—just a huge, smoking crater in the ground, completely devoid of all life.

Tom was dead.

Chapter Six

Zebediah covered up the panel once he was done, dusting his hands clean and wiping the sweat off his forehead, looking at Ryan who was sitting by the computer, a frustrated look on his face which was now starting to show the slightest hints of a stubble growing. Zebediah grinned at him and gave him a thumbs up with a sigh of relief escaping Ryan's mouth.

"Here we go. Again. Fourth time today," Ryan muttered and pushed down on a white button, the holographic face of the AI popping up in the middle of the spaceship, Zebediah smiling sheepishly at the sight of what he'd been working so long on.

"He actually did it," Tank said, his tone unusually soft as he looked at the AI's face, a tinge of sadness in his eyes. "No way."

"Only took us three weeks of remaining stationary in space, burning through andrium," Ryan muttered, combing through his overgrown hair with his hands before rising out of the seat. "Now that it's done, can we please start moving?"

There were murmurs of agreement from the incredible number of people sitting and standing in the spaceship, many of whom whose names Zebediah either didn't know or had forgotten, since he couldn't have been bothered enough to try to remember the names of all of the people who'd accepted his offer to get them off world and to a planet where they would have a chance of survival, far away from the virus that had claimed their planet. There were more people than this on the ship but the rest of them were on the lower level, hibernating in the pods down there, since they'd agreed they would all take turns in the hibernation pods.

"ZEB-TT1," Zebediah said.

"Hello, Zee Zee," the AI responded. "Is there anything you would like me to do for you?"

Zebediah smiled at the sound of the familiar voice, one that had been obtained from recordings they'd had on their phones. "Hello,

Tom," Zebediah responded and cleared his throat. "Everything's fine. Just one thing I'd like you to do."

"What's that?"

Zebediah glanced around at the others in the ship, before directing his attention back to the AI's face which was a holographic replica of the face of Tomas Tompson. He cleared his throat before providing a response.

"Plot a course for Earth, please!

THE END